Contents

A Grin Without a Cat 4

The Giant Builder 10

Arndt's Night Underground 23

The Crystal Coffin 34

A Grin Without a Cat

An extract from Alice's Adventures in Wonderland
by Lewis Carroll

*Alice follows a talking, clothed White Rabbit down a rabbit hole and falls into
a dreamlike place where anything can happen. She drinks a drink which shrinks
her and eats a cake which makes her grow. She weeps a sea of tears and talks to
animals and birds, who are washed away. A caterpillar helps her return to her
proper size, whereupon she meets a Duchess whose baby turns into a pig
and runs away. Then, high in a nearby tree, a strange cat appears…*

THE CAT ONLY GRINNED when it saw Alice. It
looked good-natured, she thought. Still it had
VERY long claws and a great many teeth, so she felt
that it ought to be treated with respect.

"Cheshire Puss," she began timidly, as she did not
at all know whether it would like the name,

A Grin Without a Cat

and other magical stories

Compiled by Vic Parker

Miles Kelly

First published in 2012 by Miles Kelly Publishing Ltd
Harding's Barn, Bardfield End Green, Thaxted, Essex, CM6 3PX, UK

Copyright © Miles Kelly Publishing Ltd 2011

2 4 6 8 10 9 7 5 3 1

Publishing Director Belinda Gallagher
Creative Director Jo Cowan
Editorial Director Rosie McGuire
Editor Carly Blake
Senior Designer Joe Jones
Editorial Assistant Lauren White
Production Manager Elizabeth Collins
Reprographics Anthony Cambray, Stephan Davis, Jennifer Hunt

ISBN 978-1-84810-581-2

Printed in China

British Library Cataloguing-in-Publication Data
A catalogue record for this book is available from the British Library

ACKNOWLEDGEMENTS
The publishers would like to thank the following artists who have contributed to this book:

Advocate Art: Alida Massari
The Bright Agency: Marcin Piwowarski (inc. cover)
Marsela Hajdinjak

All other artwork from the Miles Kelly Artwork Bank

The publishers would like to thank the following sources for the use of their photographs:
Shutterstock: (page decorations) Dragana Francuski Tolimir
Dreamstime: (frames) Gordan

Every effort has been made to acknowledge the source and copyright holder of each picture.
Miles Kelly Publishing apologises for any unintentional errors or omissions.

Made with paper from a sustainable forest

www.mileskelly.net   info@mileskelly.net

www.factsforprojects.com

however, it only grinned a little wider. 'It's pleased so far,' thought Alice, and she went on. "Would you tell me, please, which way I ought to go from here?"

"That depends a good deal on where you want to get to," said the Cat.

"I don't much care where—" said Alice.

"Then it doesn't matter which way you go," said the Cat.

"—so long as I get SOMEWHERE," Alice added as an explanation.

"Oh, you're sure to do that," said the Cat, "if you only walk long enough."

Alice tried another question. "What sort of people live about here?"

"In THAT direction," the Cat said, waving its right paw round, "lives a Hatter, and in THAT direction," waving the other paw, "lives a March Hare. Visit either you like – they're both mad."

"But I don't want to go among mad people," Alice remarked.

"Oh, you can't help that," said the Cat, "we're all mad here. I'm mad. You're mad."

"How do you know I'm mad?" said Alice.

"You must be," said the Cat, "or you wouldn't have come here."

Alice didn't think that this proved it at all, however, she went on, "And how do you know that you're mad?"

"To begin with," said the Cat, "a dog's not mad. You grant that?"

"I suppose so," said Alice.

"Well, then," the Cat went on, "you see, a dog growls when it's angry, and wags its tail when it's pleased. Now I growl when I'm pleased, and wag my tail when I'm angry. Therefore I'm mad."

"I call it purring, not growling," said Alice.

"Call it what you like," said the Cat. "Do you play croquet with the queen today?"

"I should like it very much," said Alice, "but I haven't been invited yet."

"You'll see me there," said the Cat, and vanished.

Alice was not much surprised at this, she was getting so used to queer things happening. While she was looking at the place where it had been, it suddenly appeared again.

"By-the-bye, what became of the baby?" said the Cat. "I'd nearly forgotten to ask.'

"It turned into a pig," Alice quietly said, just as if it had come back in a natural way.

"I thought it would," said the Cat, and vanished again.

Alice waited a little, half expecting to see it again, but it did not appear, and after a minute or two she walked on in the direction in which the March Hare was said to live. "I've seen hatters before," she said to herself, "the March Hare will be much the most interesting, and perhaps as this is May it won't be raving mad – at least not so mad as it was in March."

As she said this, she looked up, and there was the Cat again, sitting on a branch of a tree.

"Did you say pig, or fig?" said the Cat.

"I said pig," replied Alice, "and I do wish that you wouldn't keep appearing and vanishing so very suddenly – you make one quite giddy."

"All right," said the Cat, and this time it vanished quite slowly, beginning with the end of the tail, and ending with the grin, which remained some time after the rest of it had gone.

'Well! I've often seen a cat without a grin,' thought Alice, 'but a grin without a cat! It's the most curious thing I ever saw in my life!'

The Giant Builder

A Norse tale from *In the Days of Giants*
by Abbie Farwell Brown

AGES AND AGES AGO, when the world was first made, the gods decided to build a beautiful city high above the heavens, the most glorious and wonderful city that ever was known. Asgard was to be its name, and it was to stand on Ida Plain under the shade of Yggdrasil, the great tree whose roots were underneath the earth.

First of all they built a house with a silver roof, where there were seats for all the twelve chiefs. In the midst, and high above the rest, was the wonder throne of Odin the All-Father, whence he could see everything that happened in the sky or on the earth or in the sea. Next they made a fair house for Queen Frigg and her lovely daughters. Then they built a smithy, with great hammers, tongs, anvils, and bellows, where the gods could work at their favourite trade, the making of beautiful things out of gold, which they did so well that folk name that time the Golden Age. Afterward, as they had more leisure, they built separate houses for all the Æsir, each more beautiful than the preceding, for of course they were continually growing more skilful.

They saved Father Odin's palace until the last, for they meant this to be the largest and the most splendid of all. Gladsheim, the home of joy, was the name of Odin's house, and it was built all of gold, set in the midst of a wood whereof the trees had leaves of ruddy gold – like an autumn-gilded forest. For the safety of All-Father it was surrounded by a roaring river and by a high picket fence, and there was a great courtyard within. The glory of

Gladsheim was its wondrous hall, radiant with gold,
the most lovely room that time has ever seen.
Valhalla, the Hall of Heroes, was the name of it, and
it was roofed with the mighty shields of warriors.
The ceiling was made of interlacing spears, and
there was a portal at the west end before which
hung a great grey wolf, while over him a fierce eagle
hovered. The hall was so huge that it had five

hundred and forty gates, through each of which eight hundred men could march abreast. Indeed, there needed to be room, for this was the hall where every morning Odin received all the brave warriors who had died in battle on the earth below, and there were many heroes in those days. A happy life it was for the heroes, and a happy life for all who dwelled in Asgard, for this was before trouble had come among the gods, following the mischief of Loki.

This is how the trouble began. From the beginning of time, the giants had been unfriendly to the Æsir, because the giants were older and huger and more wicked. Besides, they were jealous because the good Æsir were fast gaining more wisdom and power than the giants had ever known. The giants hated the Æsir, and tried all in their power to injure them and the men of the earth below, whom the Æsir loved and cared for. The gods had already built a wall around Midgard, the world of men, to keep the giants out. Between Asgard and the giants flowed Ifing, the great river on which ice never formed, and which the gods crossed on the rainbow bridge. But this was not protection enough.

So the word went forth in Asgard: "We must build a fortress against the giants – the hugest, strongest, finest fortress that ever was built."

Now one day soon after, there came a mighty man stalking up the rainbow bridge that led to Asgard city.

"Who goes there!" cried Heimdal the watchman, whose eyes were so keen that he could easily see for one hundred miles around, and whose ears were so sharp that he could hear the grass growing in the meadow and the wool on the backs of the sheep. "Who goes there! There is no person who may enter Asgard if I say no."

"I am a builder," said the stranger, who was a huge fellow with sleeves rolled up to show the iron muscles of his arms. "I am a builder of strong towers, and I have heard that the folk of Asgard need one to help them raise a fair fortress in their city."

Heimdal looked at the stranger narrowly, for there was something about him which his sharp eyes did not like. But he made no answer, only blew on his golden horn, which was so loud that it sounded through all the world. At this signal all the Æsir came running to the rainbow bridge, from wherever they happened to be, to find out who it was that was coming to Asgard.

"In three half-years," declared the stranger, "I will build for you a castle so strong that not even the giants, should they swarm hither over Midgard – not even they could enter without your leave."

"Aha!" cried Father Odin, well pleased at this offer. "And what reward do you ask, friend, for help so timely?"

"I will name my price, friends," the stranger said, "a small price for so great a deed. I ask you to give me Freia for my wife, and those two sparkling jewels, the Sun and Moon."

At this demand the gods looked grave, for Freia was their dearest treasure. She was the most beautiful maid who ever lived, the light and life of heaven, and if she should leave Asgard, joy would go with her, while the Sun and Moon were the light and life of the Æsir's children, men, who lived in the little world below.

But Loki the sly whispered that they would be

safe enough if they made another condition on their part, so hard that the builder could not fulfil it. After thinking cautiously, he spoke for them all.

"Mighty man," quoth he, "we are willing to agree to your price – upon one condition. We cannot wait three half-years for our castle. See that you finish the fort without help in one winter – one short winter – and you shall have fair Freia with the Sun and Moon. But if, on the first day of summer, one stone is wanting to the walls, then you shall depart without payment."

At first the stranger shook his head and frowned, saying that in so short a time no one unaided could complete the undertaking. At last he made another offer. "Let me have but my good horse, Svadilföri, to help me with the task, and I will try," he urged. "Surely, you will not deny me this little help, from one four-footed friend."

Then again the Æsir consulted, but again Loki urged them to accept. "Surely, there is no harm," he said. "Even with an old horse to help them, no one could build the castle in the promised time. We shall gain a fortress without trouble and with never a price to pay."

Loki was so very eager that, although the other Æsir did not really agree with this crafty way of making bargains, they finally consented. Then the stranger and the Æsir gave solemn promise that the bargain should be kept.

On the first day of winter the strange builder began his work, and wondrous was the way he set about it. His strength seemed as the strength of a hundred men. As for his horse Svadilföri, he did more work by half than even the mighty builder. In the night he dragged the enormous rocks that were to be used in building the castle, rocks as big as mountains of the earth, while in the daytime the stranger piled them into place with his iron arms. The Æsir watched him with amazement, never was seen such strength in Asgard.

As the work went on, the gods began to look at one another uneasily. Who was this mighty one who had come among them, and what if after all he should win his reward? Freia trembled in her palace, and the Sun and Moon grew dim with fear.

Eventually the Æsir held a meeting upon Ida Plain, a meeting full of fear and anger. At last they realised what they had done – they had made a bargain with one of the giants, their enemies, and if he won the prize, it would mean sorrow and darkness in heaven and upon earth.

"It is your counsels, Loki, that have brought this danger upon us," quoth Father Odin, frowning. "If you cannot save for us Freia and the Sun and Moon, you shall die. This is my word." All the other Æsir agreed that this was just.

Loki was much frightened. "It was my fault, but how was I to know that he was a giant?" he cried. Then his face brightened. "Ha! I have a thought! The builder shall not finish the gate – the giant shall not receive his payment. I will cheat the fellow."

Now it was the last night of winter, and there remained but a few stones to put in place on the top of the gateway. The giant was sure of his prize, and chuckled to himself as he went out with his horse to drag the remaining stones. However, hardly had he gone to work when out of the wood came running a pretty little mare, who neighed to Svadilföri as if inviting the tired horse to leave his work and come to the green fields. Giving a snort of disobedience, off Svadilföri ran after this new friend toward the meadows. Off went the giant after him, howling with rage, as he saw his chance of success slipping out of reach. It was a mad chase, and all Asgard thundered with the noise of galloping hoofs and the giant's mighty tread. The mare was Loki in disguise, and he led Svadilföri far out of reach, to a hidden meadow, so that the giant howled and panted up and down all night, without catching a sight of his horse.

Now when the morning came the gateway was

still unfinished, and night and winter had ended at the same hour. The giant's time was over, and he had forfeited his reward.

The delighted Æsir came flocking to the gateway.

"You have failed, fellow," judged Father Odin sternly, "Leave Asgard quickly, we have seen all we want of you and of your race."

Then the giant knew that he was discovered, and he was mad with rage. "It was a trick!" he bellowed, assuming his own proper form, which was huge as a mountain, and towered high beside the fortress that he had built. "I will demolish your shining city!" But at this moment Thor, the mighty thunder god, came rushing to the rescue in his chariot of goats. Before the giant knew what had happened, his head was rolling upon the ground at Father Odin's feet, for with one blow Thor had saved Asgard.

In this extraordinary way the noble city of Asgard was made safe and complete by the addition of a fortress. But always at the top of the gate were lacking three great stones that no one was mighty enough to lift. This was a reminder to the Æsir that now they had the race of giants for their everlasting enemies. And though Loki's trick had saved them Freia, and for the world the Sun and Moon, it was the beginning of trouble in Asgard which lasted as long as Loki lived to make mischief with his guile.

Arndt's Night Underground

From *Tales of Wonder Every Child Should Know*
by Kate Douglas Wiggin and
Nora Archibald Smith

IT WAS ON A DREARY winter's night that two poor children were coming home from their daily work. Arndt and Reutha were very tired, and as they came across the moor the wind blew in their faces.

"Dear Arndt, let me sit down and rest for a minute, I can go no farther," said Reutha, as she sank down on a little mound that seemed to rise up invitingly, with its shelter of bushes.

It was not a cold night, so Arndt wrapped his sister up in her woollen cloak, and she sat down.

"I will just run a little farther and try if I can see the light in Father's window," said Arndt. "You will not be afraid, Reutha?"

"Oh, no! I am never afraid," said Reutha, and leaned her head against a branch which seemed to her as soft and inviting as a pillow.

Arndt went a little way, until he saw the light which his father always placed to guide the children over the moor. Then he felt quite safe, and went back cheerfully to his sister.

Reutha was not there! Beside the little mound and among the bushes did poor Arndt search in terror, but he could not find his sister. He called her name loudly – there was no answer. Not a single trace of her could be found, and yet he had not been five minutes away.

"Oh! What shall I do?" sobbed the boy, and there

for a long time did Arndt sit by the hillock, wringing his hands in vain.

At last there passed by an old man, who travelled about the country selling ribbons and cloths. Arndt burst into tears and told him of all that had happened that night.

The peddler's face grew graver and graver. "Arndt," whispered he, "did you ever hear of the Hill-men? It is they who have carried little Reutha away." And then the old man told how in his youth he had heard tales of this same moor, for that the little mound was a fairy-hill, where the underground dwarfs lived, and where they often carried off young children to be their servants, taking them under the hill, and only leaving behind their shoes. "For," said the peddler, "the Hill-people are very particular, and will make all their servants wear beautiful glass shoes instead of clumsy leather."

So he and Arndt searched about the hill, and there, sure enough, they found Reutha's tiny shoes hidden under the long grass. At this her brother's tears burst forth afresh.

"Oh! What shall I do to bring back my poor sister? The Hill-men and women will kill her!"

"No," said the old man, "they will keep Reutha with them a hundred years, and when she comes back you will be dead and buried, while she is still a beautiful child." And then, to comfort the boy, the peddler told him wonderful stories of the riches and splendour of the Hill-people, how that sometimes they had been seen dancing at night on the mounds, and how they wore green caps, which, if any mortal man could get possession of, the dwarfs were obliged to serve him and obey him in everything.

All this Arndt drank in with eager ears, and when the peddler went away he sat a long time thinking.

"I will do it," at last he said aloud. "I will try to get my dear Reutha safe back again."

And the boy stole noiselessly to the mound where the Hill-men were supposed to dwell. He hid himself among the surrounding bushes, and there he lay in the silence and darkness. At last a sudden brightness flashed upon the boy's eyes, the grassy hill opened, and the boy saw a palace underground, glittering with gold and gems. The Hill-men danced about within it, dressed like tiny men and women. One by one they rose out of the opening, and gambolled on the snow-covered mound, but wherever they trod flowers sprang up, and the air grew light and warm as summer. After a while they ceased dancing and began ball-playing, tossing their little green caps about in great glee. And lo and behold! One of these wonderful caps, being tossed farther than usual, lighted on the very forehead of the peeping boy! In a moment he snatched it and held on to it fast, with a cry of triumph. The light faded – the scene vanished – only Arndt heard a small weak voice whispering, humbly and beseechingly in his ear.

"Please, noble gentleman, give me my cap again."

"No, no, good Hill-man," answered the boy, in a strong, courageous voice. "You have got my little sister, and I have got your cap, which I shall keep."

"I will give you a better cap for it – all gold and jewels – oh, so beautiful!" said the Hill-man, persuasively.

"I will not have it. What good would it do me? No, no, I am your master, good dwarf, as you very well know, and I command you to take me down in the hill with you, for I want to see Reutha."

Then Arndt saw the elfin mound open again, but this time the palace was at the bottom of what looked like a dim, gloomy staircase. On the top stair stood the little Hill-man, holding a glowworm lamp, and making many low bows to his new master. Arndt glanced rather fearfully down the staircase, but then he thought of Reutha, and his love for her made him grow bold. He took upon himself a lordly air, and bade his little servant lead the way.

The Hill-man took him through beautiful

galleries, and halls, and gardens, until the boy's senses were overwhelmed with these lovely things. Every now and then he stopped, and asked for Reutha, but then there was always some new chamber to be seen, or some dainty banquet to be tasted, until, by degrees, Arndt's memory of his little sister grew dimmer. When night came, the boy felt himself lulled by sweet music to a soft dreaminess, which was all the sleep that was needed in that fairy paradise.

Thus, day after day passed in all gay delights, the elfin people were the merriest in the world, and they did all their little master desired. And Arndt knew not that while they surrounded him with delights it was only to make him forget his errand.

But one day, when the boy lay on a green dell in the lovely fairy-garden, he heard a low, wailing song, and saw a troop of little mortal children at work in the distance. Some were digging ore, and others making jewellery, while a few stood in the stream that ran by, beating linen, as it seemed. And among these poor little maidens, who worked so hard and sang so mournfully, was his own sister Reutha.

"No one cares for me," she murmured, and her song had in it a plaintive sweetness, very different from the way in which the little maiden spoke on earth. "Poor Reutha is quite alone!"

Even amidst the spells of fairyland that voice went to the brother's heart. He called the Hill-people and bade them bring Reutha to him. Then he kissed her, and wept over her, and dressed her in his own beautiful robes, while the Hill-men dared not interfere. Arndt took his sister by the hand, and said: "Now, let us go – we have stayed here long enough. Good Hill-man, you shall have your cap again when you have brought Reutha and me to our own father's door."

But the Hill-man shook his tiny head, and made his most obsequious bow. "Noble master, anything but this! This little maid we found asleep on our hill, and she is ours for a hundred years."

Here Arndt got into a passion, for, convinced of the power the little green cap gave him over the dwarfs, he had long lost all fear of them. He stamped with his foot until the little man leaped up a yard high and begged and pleaded with his master to be more patient.

"How dare you keep my sister!" cried the boy, his former companion becoming at once hateful to him. And Arndt folded his arms around Reutha and walked with her through all the gorgeous rooms, the Hill-men and women following behind and luring him with their sweetest songs, most bewitching smiles and promises of great riches and treasures. But Reutha's voice and Reutha's smile had greatest power of all over her brother's heart.

They climbed the gloomy staircase, and stood at the opening in the hillock. Arndt felt the breezes of earth playing on his cheek. How sweet they were, even after the fragrant airs of elfin-land!

"Kind master, give me my cap!" piteously implored the Hill-man.

"Take it, and goodbye for ever more!" cried Arndt, as he clasped his sister in his arms and leaped out. The chasm closed, and the two children found themselves lying in a snow-drift, with the grey dawn of a winter's morning just breaking over them.

"Where have you been all night, my children?" cried the anxious mother, as they knocked at the door.

Had it, indeed, been only a single night – the months that seemed to have passed while they were under the hill? They could not tell, for they were now like all other children, and their wisdom learned in fairyland had passed away. It seemed only a dream, save that the brother and sister loved each other better than ever, and so they continued to do as long as they lived.

The Crystal Coffin

From Andrew Lang's *Green Fairy Book*

A YOUNG TAILOR once found himself lost in a wood. Evening came on and, for fear of wild beasts, he climbed a tall oak tree. After passing several hours in fear, he noticed a light shining in the distance. Cautiously, he climbed down and went towards it.

The tailor found it came

from a house, and he knocked bravely at the door. It was opened by an old man who said roughly: "Who are you, and what do you want?"

"I beg you to let me shelter in your hut till morning," replied the youth.

Very grudgingly, the old man let him come in, and after giving him some bread and water, showed him to a bed in one corner of the room.

The weary tailor slept sound till early morning, when he was roused by a thunderous, bellowing noise. The tailor hurried out to find a huge black bull fighting with a fine large stag. At length, the stag drove his antlers with such force into his opponent's body that the bull fell to the ground, finished. Then, to the tailor's great amazement, the stag bounded up to him, forked him up with its great antlers, and set off at full gallop over hill and dale. The tailor could do nothing but hold on tight and hope for the best!

At length the stag paused before a steep rock and let the tailor down to the ground. With his antlers, he struck such a blow on a door in the rock that it flew open. Flames rushed forth and clouds of steam. The tailor was frozen with fear, but a voice from the rock cried: "Step in, no harm shall befall you."

Passing through the door, the tailor was amazed to find himself in a hall, whose ceiling, walls, and floor were covered with carved tiles. He heard the same voice saying: "Tread on the stone in the middle of the hall, and good luck will attend you."

Hardly had he stepped on the stone than it began to sink with him into the depths below. He found himself in an even more splendid hall, whose walls were lined with shelves on which stood glass vessels filled with bright-coloured smokes. On the floor were two large crystal boxes opposite each other, and these attracted his curiosity at once.

Stepping up to one, he saw within it a model castle surrounded by farms, barns, stables, and a number of other buildings. Everything was quite tiny, but perfect.

He was even more amazed at what was in the other crystal box. Lying there was a beautiful girl. She looked asleep, but though her eyes were closed, the bright colour in her face, and the movement of a ribbon, which rose and fell with her breath, left no doubt as to her being alive.

Suddenly the maiden opened her eyes and started with delight. "Help me!" she cried. "Only push back the bolt of this coffin and I am free from my prison."

The tailor promptly obeyed, and the girl quickly pushed back the crystal lid and stepped out. After giving her rescuer a kiss to thank him, she explained: "I am the daughter of a wealthy nobleman. My parents died when I was very young, and they left me to the care of my eldest brother, whom I love very much. One evening, a stranger rode up to the castle and asked for shelter. Of course, we took him in. But that night, I woke to find the stranger entering my room, even though the door had been locked. He was softly singing a strange song, and I found I could neither move nor cry out! Then I must have fainted, for I remember nothing more until I opened my eyes to find myself lying here, in this crystal coffin. The magician – for that is indeed what the stranger was – appeared again and told me that he had transformed my brother into a wild stag. He had shrunk our castle and the surrounding village to miniature and locked them up in another glass box. And after turning everyone in our household into smoke, had banished them into glass jars. He told me that if I agreed to marry him, he would undo all the spells! He said he would leave me time to ponder my fate and he vanished. Now, to my great joy, you are here – and now I beg you to help me again, to save my people."

The tailor and the maiden lifted the glass box

containing the models onto the stone in the middle of the hall. The stone gently transported them all into the upper hall, from where they easily carried the box outside. The lady then removed the lid, and the castle, houses, and farmyards grew and spread themselves till they had regained their proper size. Then the young couple brought up all the glass vessels filled with smoke. No sooner were they uncorked than brightly-coloured clouds billowed out of them and became all the lady's servants and attendants.

The maiden's joy was complete when her brother came from the forest in his proper shape. Of course, he had been the stag, and he had killed the magician – who had been in the form of the bull. That very day, the lady gave her hand in marriage to the young tailor, and they lived happily ever after.